The
Witch's Ring

The
Witch's Ring

Rachel Dixon

Illustrated by Jennifer Hewitson

Hyperion Books for Children
New York

First Hyperion Books for Children edition 1994
Text © 1992 by Rachel Dixon.
Illustrations © 1994 by Jennifer Hewitson.
First published in 1992 by Doubleday, a division of Transworld Publishers Ltd.,
61–63 Uxbridge Road, London W5 5SA, United Kingdom.
Printed in the United States of America.
For information address Hyperion Books for Children,
114 Fifth Avenue, New York, New York 10011.

1 3 5 7 9 10 8 6 4 2

Library of Congress Cataloging-in-Publication Data
Dixon, Rachel Taft.
The witch's ring / Rachel Dixon; illustrated by Jennifer Hewitson - 1st ed.
p. cm.
"First published in 1992 by Doubleday" - T.p. verso.
Summary: A curious boy named Bottle uses his computer
to help Amy Settle find her way home after a magical ring
transports her to the home of an evil witch.
ISBN 1-56282-545-3 — ISBN 1-56282-546-1 (lib. bdg.)
[1.Witches — Fiction. 2. Magic — Fiction. 3. Computers — Fiction.]
I. Hewitson, Jennifer, ill. II. Title
PZ7.D6465Wi 1994 [Fic] — dc20 93-34192 CIP AC

For Emily
—R. D.

The
Witch's Ring

Chapter One

If it hadn't been for James Bone I would never have met the witch. He was a nasty boy from the end of our street, who kept shouting rude names at me over our front garden wall. He usually caught me off guard, but that morning I was ready for him.

I sat on the wall, waiting. It was a good wall, wide enough to keep your balance and high enough to see down the street in both directions. There was no sign of James Bone yet, but I knew he would come eventually. He always did.

I could see two crows in the opposite gutter, pecking at something squashed there. They flapped away whenever a car came past, but only just in time. I was hoping they would be gone for good by the time James Bone came, because he was the sort of boy who would throw something at a bird for fun. And he wouldn't miss.

I saw James Bone before he saw me. He was approaching from the direction of his house, gliding skillfully along the pavement on his skateboard. That was typical of him, to have wheels to escape on. The coward.

I slid off the wall into our front garden. It was an ideal place to hide, concealed from the house by a laurel bush and hidden from the road by the wall itself. Down beside me were two Squeaky Clean dishwashing-liquid bottles filled to the top with cold water. I held one firmly in each hand and waited.

James Bone reached the wall very quickly and scraped to a halt. I didn't feel so brave now that he was there, a mere brick's-width away.

"Amy Settle," he called. "Where are you?"

I kept very quiet, my hands gripping the Squeaky Clean bottles.

"I know you're there, Settle," he said.

I felt sick to my stomach. Could he see me?

"Amy Settle, looks like a kettle," he chanted. "And she's got a tongue like a stinging nettle."

That did it. He'd asked for it now. I sprang up from behind the wall, took aim, and squeezed. It was incredible. Better than I could ever have hoped for. Water curved out of the Squeaky Clean bottles in perfect arcs and hit James Bone right in the face.

He stood there for a moment, shocked, and the water kept on coming. By the time he had the sense to back out of range, his head and shoulders were drenched.

"You're going to get it now, Amy Settle," he said nastily.

Then I did the worst thing possible. I laughed. I couldn't help it. He looked just like a wet dog, standing there shaking his dripping hair.

"I'm going, Amy Settle," he said, pushing off on his skateboard with great dignity.

"But I'll be back."

He was back sooner than I expected. I had only just had time to refill my Squeaky Clean bottles and return to my hiding place when I heard a noise on the other side of the wall. The beast. He'd crept up the street while I was in the house.

I crouched low and grasped the bottles firmly

in my hands. He slowly came nearer, moving so close to the wall that I could see the top of his head right above where I was hiding.

He'd have a weapon this time for sure. There was nothing to do but attack first. I rose swiftly, with my eyes shut, and squeezed the bottles hard.

"Take that, James Bone," I said.

The caps burst off both bottles, sloshing cold bubbly water all over me.

"Now look what you've made me do, Bone," I said, crouching down and trying to blink the bubbles out of my eyelashes.

"Bone?" said an indignant voice.

I stood. Facing me, on the opposite side of the wall, was a girl of about my height. The water had hit her, too, and her hair was drenched.

"How *dare* you do this to me?" she said furiously. She had straight hair and blue eyes and reminded me of someone I knew.

"You shouldn't go spying over people's walls," I said.

Then I did it again. I laughed. And once I'd started, I couldn't stop.

"Shut up," she said. "I never thought *this* would happen. You've ruined my day, that's what you've done. And I hate you."

"I'm sorry," I said, trying not to smile. "You shouldn't have sneaked up on me like that. I thought you were James Bone."

She scowled at me so angrily that her eyebrows nearly swapped sides.

"Why don't you come inside," I said, "and I'll lend you a towel."

Her expression changed suddenly. She looked toward the house, interested.

"I'll come inside if you let me see your room," she said.

"You're not seeing my room until you stop being angry with me," I said.

The girl smiled stiffly, like someone whose mouth was out of practice.

"OK," she said.

So I took her indoors.

Chapter Two

We went up to my bedroom. It was a pretty room with striped blue wallpaper. We sat on the bed and rubbed our wet hair with towels.

"I'm Amy Settle," I said. "What's your name?"

She said nothing. She *was* still angry with me.

"If you look down the garden you can see my mom," I said. "She's playing with my little brother. His name is Toby."

"How old is he?" she said from behind her towel.

"Two," I said. "And he's really sweet."

"My brother's older than me," she said. "And I hate him. That's one of the reasons why I've left home."

"I thought children who left home packed a case and took their favorite teddy with them," I said.

"I didn't have time to pack," she said. "And I don't have a teddy. They're stupid."

"What will your mom say?"

"Nothing," she said. "I live with my grandma Ethel. She's horrible. She keeps asking me to do chores when I want to play."

"She can't be that bad," I said, thinking fondly of my own grandmothers.

"Well, she is," said the girl sharply. "She's a nasty old witch."

She let the towel drop to the floor and began to walk around my room, touching things. I was beginning to wish I hadn't invited her in. She wasn't very nice at all. Imagine her talking about her grandma like that!

"I'm going to need some dry clothes," said the girl, opening my closet without asking. She pulled out my favorite pink jumpsuit and a white belt. "This should do."

Before I could argue, she had slipped out of her dress and into *my* clothes.

"Amazing," she said, admiring herself in the mirror. "I look just like you now."

She smiled again. But it was an odd smile that made me shiver.

"Why don't you try my dress on, Amy Settle?" she said. "It's not too wet *really*."

I shook my head.

"Go on," said the girl, smiling again. "Just for fun."

I picked up her dress. It was a very pretty design made up with bright soft cotton, and it fit perfectly.

"Now I'm Amy Settle," she said. "And you are me. If you went back to my house, I bet Grandma Ethel wouldn't even notice the difference."

"Of course she would," I said angrily. "I'm *quite* different."

"Not very," said the girl, pulling me up to the mirror. "Have a look in here."

We stood close to each other with our arms by our sides. She was right. We were very similar, uncannily so.

"Only the hair's different," said the girl, "but you could easily straighten yours if you wanted to."

"Do you think so?" I said. "Yours is very pretty."

"Of course," she said. "And I could make mine curly if I wanted to."

She put her hands into her pockets, as if feeling for something.

"Oh no!" she said. "It's gone."

"What is?"

"My ring. I'm sure I put it in my pocket . . . and now it's not there."

"Don't be silly," I said. "You're wearing *my* clothes. It must be in this dress pocket."

"Oh yes," she said. "How stupid of me. Get it out, would you?"

I found the ring and pulled it out. It was a wide gold band with a beautifully etched design of leaves and flowers.

"Wow!" I said. "It's beautiful. Who does it belong to?"

"It's mine," she said. "You can try it on if you like."

I slid it on to my finger.

"There's writing on it," said the girl. "Can you read it?"

I peered closely at the delicate design. She was right. Set in among the leaves and flowers were six tiny letters.

"Gemini," I said.

The moment I uttered the word, something

very strange began to happen. A tingly sensation spread from my toes to my head, and the girl beside me began to fade from view. She was disappearing, getting smaller. No . . . *she* hadn't changed, not unless the closet had shrunk, too. It was *me* that was moving, slowly at first, then faster and faster, whizzing away from my room at great speed.

Where was I going? There were colors, noises, and blurred shapes flashing past me, but nothing I could make out until, a few minutes later, I flopped down into a lumpy armchair.

Chapter Three

I was in a gloomy candle-lit room. Against the wall on the left there was a table, and sitting at it, with her back to me, was a very old woman, dressed in black. Her bony shoulders were hunched over a big book in which she wrote laboriously with an old-fashioned quill pen.

"And what have you got to say for yourself?" she asked, still writing.

"Pardon?"

The lumps in the armchair wriggled, and a thin black cat clawed its way indignantly out from under me. It jumped to the floor and scratched itself revoltingly.

"I thought I told you to keep out of my room," said the old woman. Her pen stopped for a moment.

She turned her attention to her writing again,

chanting as she wrote: "*One bat's tooth . . . a pinch of snuff . . . toenail of . . .*"

"Excuse me," I said. "But I don't know you."

"*Toenail of . . . slug?* No, that can't be right. I'll put *bug.*"

"My name is Amy Settle," I said. "And I've never seen you before in my life."

The old woman turned sharply. Her nose hooked over the back of the chair like an umbrella handle. The moment I saw her face, I knew she was a witch. I felt a crawling sensation all over me as I remembered the girl's words: "I live with my grandma Ethel. She's a nasty old witch."

"Don't you start your pretending with me, young lady," said the witch. "I know my own granddaughter when I see her. Leaky Kettle, indeed. What bunk. Your name is Castanetta, and I expect it always has been."

She turned back to her writing. The cat jumped onto the corner of the table and sat watching me with mean yellow eyes.

"*Fresh leaf of viper's bugloss . . .*"

I stood shakily and looked around. Now that my eyes were getting accustomed to the dimness, I could recognize some of the cluttered shapes around the room. Against the opposite wall, with its head pushed into the corner, was a rumpled bed above which was a black-curtained window. On the walls were piles of moldy old books on rickety shelves, shanks of seaweed on hooks, strings of chalky stones with holes in them, and bunches of dried herbs. On the floor were stacks of fluorescent police cones and boxes of police helmets, jars of colored feathers, and smelly cages with things that squeaked in them.

Under the table, held firmly between the witch's feet, was a large wooden bowl with a carved lid.

"Sit down, Castanetta," said the witch, without turning. "You're not going anywhere until you've apologized. You stole my ring. I knew it was missing the moment I stepped in here . . . *eye of octopus* . . . no, I'll never get that at this time of year . . . *eye of potato*."

"But I haven't done anything," I said angrily. "And I'm *not* Castanetta!"

"I might have known you'd come up with an excuse like that . . . *sliver of slime . . . and a garnish of gunk*."

"But it's *not* an excuse," I said. "I'm *me*. Look

at me carefully and you'll see the difference. I've met Castanetta all right, and I don't like her. She sent me here on purpose, and it's not very funny."

The witch peered over the back of her chair again.

"Well?" I said. "Can you spot the difference?"

"No," she said, "but your hair's a mess."

I opened my mouth to try to explain, but she silenced me with a look.

"And now," she said, "I think I'll have my ring back."

She stood stiffly and held out a gnarled hand like a claw.

"No," I said. "I want to go home. I don't like it here."

"Enough!" said the witch.

Her eyes hardened and she pointed toward me with a knobby finger. I held my breath, convinced she was about to turn me into something nasty. Instead, I felt a sharp burning sensation where the ring had been and looked down to see that it had gone.

"Got it," said the witch, triumphantly twirling it on her finger. "I haven't lost my touch, have I? They all thought I was past my prime, but I've still got what it takes. And they'll soon know it when I finish my potion . . . my life's work." She put the ring in her palm and peered at it for a moment before sinking down in her chair, exhausted. "I'm sure I can't remember what I used to use it for, but it's very pretty, isn't it? Put it back safe and sound, Ethel . . . that's the best thing to do. Put it out of harm's way. . . ."

She rocked backward and forward on her chair, so that her long gray hair flopped out of its halfhearted bun at the back of her head.

"Hide away, hide away," she crooned.

She picked up the startled cat that crouched on her table and cradled it like a baby.

All this time she had kept the ring firmly clutched in her bony hand, but at least for the moment she seemed to have forgotten I was there. I tiptoed stealthily toward the door, slid down the handle, pulled it open . . . and stepped outside.

Chapter Four

I had no idea what horrors I might discover outside the witch's room, so I was very relieved to find that I was on an ordinary upstairs landing, much like the one at home. There were five doors leading off it, including the witch's, and opposite me was a flight of stairs, curving down to a big front door.

I stepped silently on the top stair. The front door below me was my escape route, and it was so close that in just a minute I'd be free.

"Stop right there," said a voice behind me.

It was the witch.

I tried to move, but my legs felt funny.

"Turn and look at me," she said, her voice rasping like a wood saw.

I felt myself turn. She stood in her doorway, ancient and bowed. In one arm she held the balding cat and with the other she shielded her dark eyes from the light.

"You may have escaped punishment for stealing my ring," she said, "but you will certainly not leave this house until you have collected the ingredients I asked for."

"I don't know what you mean," I said.

"Of course you do. You can start by looking around the damp floorboard in your bedroom."

I nodded helplessly.

"And don't even *think* of trying to escape," she said. "There is no way out. No door or window in this house will open again until *I* decide it."

I was trapped.

"And if you ever set foot in my room again, be you Castanetta or be you not, I will cast such a spell on you that you will wish you had never been born. And the same goes for that brother of yours. I knew you two weren't to be trusted."

She hobbled back into her room, leaving me alone on the landing.

On my right was the bathroom, and on my left were three other doors, all closed. I knew that behind one of them was Castanetta's bedroom, the room with a damp floorboard. *But what was behind the others?*

I walked down the landing, took a deep breath, and opened the first door.

Chapter Five

*W*arm sunlight flooded out of the room, and inside I could see a very different sort of clutter from that in the witch's room. There were bright books, videocassettes, lots of pens and pencils, balls of colored string, model kits, and posters.

Thinking it must be Castanetta's room, I stepped inside and shut the door.

But someone was there.

"Go away, Castanetta," said an irritated voice.

On the far side of the room, at a place that had been hidden from my view by the door, was a computer desk. Sitting at the desk, with his back to me, was a fair-haired boy. He took a disk out of his computer and replaced it with another.

"Hello," I said.

"If that's your way of apologizing," he said, keying a command on the screen, "you can forget it. You're lucky she let you out alive."

"I don't think you understand," I said. "My name is Amy Settle."

He turned sharply.

"Come off it, Castanetta," he said. "You'll have to think of something better than that. You don't really expect to fool anybody into thinking a *nice* girl has miraculously arrived in your place by simply changing your name, do you?"

He turned back to the screen.

"Darn," he said. "It's not reading the disk."

He rekeyed the command.

"I'm *not* Castanetta," I said. "But I've met her all right. She's a mean and selfish girl, and she sent me here on purpose so you and your grandma could be horrible to me."

He ignored me.

"Look at me, will you?" I said. "Can't you see the difference?"

He turned angrily.

"No," he said, "but your hair looks awful."

"Please," I said. "You've got to believe me."

"No, I don't," he said, turning back to the screen. "You've made a fool of me once too often. I'm never going to fall for one of *your* tricks again. And you needn't think I'm going to help you collect the stuff for Grandma, either.

Just bug off, will you. You've even made my computer crash."

"I'd better go then," I said.

"Good."

"By the way."

"What?"

"I think you'll find you've put the disk in upside down."

That sentence changed everything. The boy spun around, wearing a strange expression.

"What did you say?" he said.

"I just said that I thought you might have put the disk in upside down. Either that or you might have made a mistake with the command. It's easily done. You've got to get all the spaces and things right, or the computer won't recognize it . . . but then you already know that, don't you?"

"Yes," he said, puzzled. "But *you* don't."

"Castanetta might not," I said haughtily, "but I've been using my mom's computer since I was five."

There was a long silence.

"So you're not Castanetta then," he said, peering at me with renewed interest.

I shook my head.

"And I've just been shouting at a complete stranger?"

"Yes."

He gave me a very nice smile and held out his hand.

"My name's Bottle," he said. "Sorry."

"That's all right," I said. "I'm Amy Settle."

Chapter Six

I went straight to his window. His room was at the front of the house, and outside I could see an ordinary street. The houses were a bit nicer than ours, mostly detached with nice front gardens, but they couldn't be far from home.

"So where did Castanetta find *you?*" said Bottle. "You look so much like her, you could almost be twins."

"Fifteen Battle Road," I said. "Is it near here?"

"I don't know. How long did it take you to get here?"

"Only a few minutes," I said. "But it's hard to tell where you're going when you travel by magic."

"By what?" Bottle looked rather pale.

"Magic," I said. "Castanetta tricked me into wearing your grandma's ring, and when I said the magic word it brought me here. She told me

she'd left home, but she needn't think *I'm* exchanging places with her. As soon as I've got the ingredients she was meant to collect, your grandma will let me out of the house. And then I'll go straight home."

"It may not be that simple," said Bottle, taking a street map from his shelf.

"Don't worry," I said. "I'm pretty good at reading maps."

"I knew it," said Bottle, running his finger anxiously down the map index. "There *is* no Battle Road."

"Of course there is."

"Not in Adderwort there isn't."

"I don't live in Adderwort," I said. "Where's your street map of Bletchindale?"

"I haven't got one," said Bottle.

"Why not?"

"I've never needed one," he said, "because if Bletchindale is where I think it is, it's about two hundred and fifty miles away."

"You're joking," I said. "Aren't you?"

He shook his head.

I sat on the edge of his bed. Stunned.

"Never mind," he said, trying to sound confident. "There must be a way around this."

He took a piggy bank from his shelf and shook it hopefully.

"I might have enough for the train fare," he said. "Or at least part of it."

"That's no good," I said. "My mom might already have discovered I'm missing. She'll be frantic."

"Not if Castanetta's little plan has worked," he said. "She won't be at all worried if she thinks you're still there."

I didn't like the sound of that.

"I'm going to call her," I said, rushing to his door. "Where's the phone?"

"I wouldn't do that," said Bottle.

"Why not? I want her to tell that sister of yours to go away. She's not going to take my place. Not even for a day."

"Don't you think it might give your mom a bit of a shock if she hears your voice on the phone, when all the time she thinks you're there in the house with her? You might make her ill. Shock does funny things to people, you know."

He was right. I sat again, my head jangling with panic.

"Well, I can't go back the way I came, can I?" I said.

"I suppose I could try to explain things to Grandma," said Bottle doubtfully, "and see if she'd let you borrow the ring for a while. I expect she'd let me in if I told her it was an emergency."

"I doubt it," I said. "She said that if either of us set foot in there again, she'd cast such a spell on us that we would wish we'd never been born."

"Oh dear," said Bottle.

"What did she mean?" I said, trying to keep the fear out of my voice.

"I don't know," he said.

"What do you mean, you don't know? She's your grandma, isn't she?"

"Yes," he said. "But we only found her a few weeks ago."

Chapter Seven

"What do you mean 'found'?" I said, trying to imagine how you could lose a grandmother in the first place.

"Last month, Mom got a phone call from a man in remotest Wolverton, saying he had discovered an elderly relative of ours living on the property of his newly built dream house."

"Where does your mom live?"

"Here."

"That's not what Castanetta said."

"She says that to try and get sympathy," said Bottle. "But Mom's only away for three weeks. She's staying with our aunt Betishka in Moscow. The man phoned her here, two weeks before she planned to leave.

"Mom assured the man that she knew the whereabouts of all of our relatives and was quite sure that none of them were in Wolverton, but the man was so insistent that she finally agreed to go over there.

"When she arrived she discovered Ethel, and, after talking to her for a while, she realized that she was our great-great-grandmother."

"She can't be," I said. "She'd have to be a hundred years old."

"She's much older than that."

"Why isn't she dead then? Nobody lives that long."

Bottle shrugged.

"It's a mystery," he said. "She went out herb gathering one day when she was about ninety, and when she failed to return everybody assumed the worst. It was quite a shock for Mom to come face-to-face with her, I tell you."

"Did she know she was a witch?"

"Oh yes," said Bottle. "She was the last known bad witch in our family."

"I thought all witches were bad."

"Quite the opposite. Aunt Betishka, the one Mom's staying with, is a witch, but it's all changed these days. They work with sophisticated computers and only do good. They study the history of spell making as part of their education, but they have to be properly registered before they can have access to the dangerous spells that were banned from use years ago."

"And your grandma doesn't know that, I suppose?"

"No," said Bottle uncomfortably. "She's been out of circulation for so long that she has no idea how things have changed. Mom said it was lucky the man who found her was kind to her, or he might not have lived to tell the tale."

"Didn't he notice her house when he bought the land?"

"It was more of a hovel than a house," said Bottle. "He discovered it when he was clearing a thicket at the bottom of his garden."

"I don't suppose that made him very happy."

"Hardly. Having an ancient witch living in his garden could have knocked thousands of dollars off the value of his house. He couldn't get much information out of Grandma except that she was working on a special recipe, so he waited until she went out berry collecting and searched her things for a clue to her identity. He managed to trace Mom from some papers he found there."

"What did your mom think of the hovel?"

"She was horrified by it. The place was

absolutely filthy, and there was no running water or electricity."

"And was your grandma happy to see her?"

"She wasn't happy at all to be disturbed, not even by a blood relation. Mom carefully explained the situation to her and told her she was welcome to come and stay in our spare room until she found another place to live, but she refused to move. It wasn't until the bulldozers arrived that she finally agreed to come.

"She kicked up a fuss, though, and put a spell on the bulldozer until she'd had time to get Mom over with a van for her belongings. She brought it all: books, animals, herbal potions, greasy old curtains, the lot. We couldn't believe the smell when we unloaded it at this end. She didn't really want us to touch anything, especially her recipe book and a funny wooden bowl. Apparently, she'd been working on a special potion for years and was very annoyed to be uprooted when she had been so close to finishing it.

"Mom had got the room really nice for her, but she insisted upon making it as much like her hovel as possible. I doubt that it will ever be cleaned again, and the curtains are permanently closed. The worst thing is that she refuses to use the electric light. We've had to put smoke detectors all over the place in case she sets something on fire with her candles."

"Your mom must really be worried."

"She is," said Bottle. "She nearly canceled her vacation. But we couldn't let her do that. She brought us up on her own and hasn't been away for years. Castanetta and I were supposed to stay with another aunt, but we said we'd stay at home instead and keep an eye on Grandma.

"The trouble is that Grandma thinks she's keeping an eye on us. She's convinced that Castanetta and I have to be kept out of trouble and gives us all sorts of chores to do, like collecting houseflies and searching for centipedes in the garden."

"Ugh! She wouldn't get me doing that."

"That's what we thought, but in the end we decided it would be safer to keep her happy. It didn't help, though. The minute we finished one task she set another. Have you ever tried buying fresh cockroaches or searching for deadly nightshade in the middle of Adderwort? It's no joke, I can tell you. Castanetta pretended to cooperate at first, but now she thinks up excuses to get me to do all the jobs. She's selfish like that."

"And I suppose you couldn't let on to your grandma?"

"No. I wasn't sure how she'd react if we made her angry. She's got some dangerous-looking things in that room of hers. So I've had to work extra hard. I'm really mad at Castanetta, of course, but she's always been irritating. In fact, everything seemed all right until this morning."

"What happened?"

"Grandma decided to go out. She doesn't leave the house very often. She says there are far too many people about these days. 'I need a rat's whisker, plucked by a witch's hand,' she said. 'But I shall not be gone for long. You will both keep away from my room while I am out. Bottle will stay in his own room, and Castanetta will gather a dozen wood lice and three large spiders.'

" 'Why me?' said Castanetta. 'Bottle never helps.'

" 'My recipe requires them to be collected by a young maiden,' said Grandma. 'I shall know if it was not done by you and will deal with you accordingly.' "

"So Castanetta had to do some of the work for a change?"

Bottle nodded.

"But she didn't. She said, 'We're not going to be bossed about by an old witch . . . *or* dealt with. *She's* the one who needs to be dealt with, and I bet there's something in her room that will help us.'"

"What did you say?"

"I offered to find the wood lice and spiders for her."

"But she wasn't interested?"

"No. She started stamping and shouting names at me. She said I was a coward and a pig and that she was going into Grandma's room whatever I thought. There was nothing I could do to stop her. She went in there and shut the door."

"And that must have been when she found the ring."

"Yes, but I'm surprised she put it on. It could have taken her anywhere."

"Not really," I said. "It has the word *Gemini* engraved on it, like the star sign. She must have guessed it was something to do with twins or look-alikes."

"I doubt it," said Bottle. "Not unless there

were some instructions with it. She probably just wanted it because it was pretty. She's silly like that."

"Whatever the reason," I said, "I've got to get it back. I want to go home, and the sooner the better."

Bottle looked at me seriously.

"There is one thing we can try," he said. "But it will be dangerous."

Chapter Eight

At eleven o'clock the witch started snoring. We could hear it quite clearly, even with Bottle's door closed.

"She's having her midmorning sleep," said Bottle. "Now's our chance."

We crept along the landing and eased the witch's door open. The only light in the room came from a single candle stump on her table.

We could see the witch lying on top of her rumpled bed with her bony ankles crossed. Her knobby arms were folded over her thin chest, and her mouth was wide open, emitting disgusting snores. By her stockinged feet lay the thin black cat, curled up in a tight ball with one paw placed firmly over his ears.

"It could be anywhere," whispered Bottle. "You look on the shelves while I check her pockets."

We stepped inside. Bottle walked over to the witch, his huge shadow moving eerily along the wall before him. I watched with morbid fascination as he leaned over her and slid his fingers slowly into each of her pockets. He shook his head. The ring wasn't there.

He joined me beside the shelves, and we looked helplessly at each other. It was impossible to know where to start. Books, pots, boxes, shoes, bunches of herbs, and an old kettle were precariously balanced there. Touch one item and everything might fall.

"She was sitting at her table when she took back her ring," I whispered. "Let's look there first."

The table was nearly as bad as the shelves, stacked high with ancient books, pots of pen points, discarded wrappers for Crunchy Cockroach Eclairs, and jam jars with unspeakable things in them. In the center was her recipe book, still open, with the flickering candle stump beside it.

Bottle pointed toward the candle. Set alone behind it was a rusty tin, its lid white with dust. He signaled for me to look in there while he lifted the lid of the carved wooden bowl beneath the table.

"It's not in here," he whispered. "It's full of petroleum jelly."

In the tin were a few small bones, three marbles, a twist of yellowing paper, and a very large beetle. When I realized that the beetle was alive, I dropped the tin. Its contents scattered over the table, knocking over the candle stump, which landed on the witch's open recipe book, splattering it with

melted wax and licking at it with a pale flame.

Bottle stood, startled. We watched transfixed as the flame grew stronger, slowly eating its way across the dry page. On the table, beside the burning book, the beetle scuttled around in circles, unable to cope with its sudden release from captivity.

"Quick!" I said. "Put out the fire!"

Bottle picked up a stack of papers and flapped it at the book, trying to snuff out the flames. Foul smoke wound up to the ceiling and rolled across toward the sleeping witch. The twist of paper from the tin was alight now, and as Bottle flapped at it, some ash fell away to reveal something shiny within its creases.

"It's the ring," I said. "Grab it."

Bottle blew on the twist until it stopped smoking, picked it up, and pushed it deep into his pocket.

All the flames were out now, leaving the room in smoky darkness. We stumbled across to the door, feeling for the handle and trying not to cough.

It was only when we reached the door that we

realized that the snoring had stopped. We stood very still. Listening.

"Bottle and Castanetta, stop right where you are," said the witch.

Chapter Nine

We kept very still.

"I know you're there," said the witch. She coughed hideously as the smoke caught in her throat. "I can smell you."

Should we make a run for it? I wondered.

"What are you doing in my room?" asked the witch.

We said nothing.

"I see," she said. "There *is* no reason. Just as I thought."

Our eyes adjusted to the smoky gloom, and we could see the dark form of the witch rising evilly from the bed. Bands of smoke drifted around her like snakes. We instinctively drew together.

"You are very naughty children," said the witch. "And you will have to be punished."

She raised her thin arms and waved them rhythmically as she chanted these words:

> Hullorum, bullorum, binkam bash,
> Thunder roar and lightning flash . . .

Smoke wafted toward us, irritating our eyes and throats. But suddenly I realized that the smoke might save us.

> Turn these beings sly and evil,
> To a natterjack toad and big boll weevil.

Not daring to take my eyes off the witch, I reached slowly behind my back until I could feel the cold door handle with one hand and the light switch with the other. The witch didn't notice. She was far too involved with her spell, pointing her hooked nose into the air and rocking from side to side like a grotesque puppet.

> Unless by chance they can persuade,
> Mighty Ethel's wrath to fade.

As she spoke these last words, I switched on the light. At the same time I pulled the door open as far as it would go. It hit Bottle's elbow.

The effect was startling. The witch, blinded by the light, sank down onto her bed. Bottle yelled at the pain in his elbow. And a moment later the smoke detector outside the room shrilled. The noise was *deafening*.

"*Aaargh!*" shrieked the witch, clutching her head. "Demons . . . save me from the demons."

The thin black cat, who had slept until now, leapt up wide eyed. It clawed its way to the top of the heavy black curtains, where it hung like a wingless bat.

"Yes, demons!" I shouted. "But I think we can save you."

I felt a tingling sensation in my feet. It was too late. The witch's spell was beginning to work. I looked down in horror to see brown webbed toes pushing out of my sneakers, splitting them open as easily as if they had been made of paper. Then I began to grow smaller. Rounder.

"Save me," moaned the witch, rocking to and fro.

Beside me, Bottle was shrinking, too. He was already as small as the cat. But he realized what I was trying to do.

"Oh no!" he cried in a strange high-pitched voice. "We're changing. We can't save you, Grandma. You're doomed."

I was smaller still. Toad sized.

"Stop your spell before it's too late," I shouted, hopping toward her on four springy legs.

The witch rose up above us, wide eyed and desperate.

"I'll change you back," she said, "if you promise to send away the demons. They hurt my head so."

I tried to speak again, but no words came. Just croaks and a long flicking tongue. Bottle was pea sized now and still shrinking, but he squeaked something that the witch seemed to understand. She pointed toward us, saying:

Stop, stop the spell that Ethel made,
For now the witch's wrath doth fade.

Again, again! I thought. It's not going to work.

But, by a miracle, it did. We grew as quickly as we had shrunk, and in half a minute we were ourselves again, standing shakily by the open door.

"Quick, Bottle!" I cried, before the witch had time to change her mind. "Let's banish the demons."

We ran out of the room, closing the door as we went.

"How do we stop it?" said Bottle, peering anxiously up at the smoke detector.

"We'll have to remove the battery," I said, reaching up to open the front of it.

"You're not supposed to, but this is an emergency."

"Hurry!" said Bottle. "She might be coming."

But it wasn't necessary. The smoke had dispersed sufficiently for the alarm to stop of its own accord, leaving our ears ringing in the sudden silence.

The witch's door burst open.

"Have they gone?" she said, eyeing us suspiciously.

"Yes, it's safe now," said Bottle. "But it wasn't easy."

I nodded.

"Where did the smoke come from?" said the witch. "I got a lungful in there. It's done me no good. You have to be careful at my age."

"Demons always come with flame and smoke," I said. "The noise only comes later."

"Yes," said Bottle. "We could smell the smoke. We feared the worst. That's why we had to come into your room. We wanted to warn you."

"Where were the flames?" she said. "I didn't see any flames."

"They'd gone by the time we came in," I said. "But you may find they've done some damage. Demons are like that."

"Damage?" said the witch anxiously. "I shall have to have a look at this damage. I've got important things in there that I don't want to be damaged."

She turned to go, and we allowed ourselves to breathe more freely.

"But just because you got away with entering my room *this* time," she said, looking back over her knobby shoulder, "don't think you can try it again, demons or no demons."

"Of course not," said Bottle obediently.

"And no one shall leave this house until my ingredients have been collected."

The witch went into her room and shut the door. We waited, hardly daring to move, and eventually heard cries from within.

"Oh, my spell, my special recipe," she moaned. "It's ruined. The demons have burned it. It will take weeks to catch up. Weeks!"

"Almost makes you feel sorry for her, doesn't it?" I said as we walked back to Bottle's room.

"Almost," said Bottle. "Until you start wondering what *that* spell is for."

Chapter Ten

Once we were back in his room, Bottle took the charred twist of paper out of his pocket. He held it carefully in the palm of his left hand and, with a finger and thumb, pulled out the Gemini ring.

"There you are," he said, passing it to me. "You'd better go home before she notices it's missing."

I took the ring and slid it on to my finger.

"I hope Castanetta hasn't caused *too* much trouble," he added.

"Me, too," I said grimly.

I took a few deep breaths to steady myself, then said the magic word.

"Gemini."

Nothing happened. I tried again with the same result.

"Say it a bit louder," said Bottle.

"Gemini!"

No luck. We looked at each other hopelessly.

"Now what?" I said.

"Are you sure you said the right word?"

"Of course I am. It's written on the ring for anybody to see."

A look of realization crossed Bottle's face.

"Perhaps that command only works for the return journey," he said. "And it's written on the ring so that whatever happens to you, you don't forget it. Castanetta should have said it, but because she got *you* to read it, the ring brought you back instead."

"You mean Castanetta had to say something else to *get* to my house?"

"Yes."

"*She's* not a witch, is she?"

"No."

"So how did she know what to say? I'm sure your grandma didn't tell her."

"It must have been written somewhere," said Bottle. "On something Grandma kept with the ring . . ." He hesitated for a moment and slowly opened his left hand to reveal the charred twist of paper. "Something like a piece of paper."

"Quick," I said. "Let's have a look at it."

We took the paper to Bottle's desk and gently placed it on a clean sheet of white computer paper.

"Look," said Bottle, carefully unwinding the twist. "It's got writing on it. And it's only damaged in places."

"There's a brown burn right down the middle," I said.

"But the left-hand side isn't too bad," said Bottle. "Perhaps we can work it out from what *is* there."

"We'll probably find it's just an old shopping list," I said gloomily.

This is what we could read:

ake me, Gemi	and and ,
To the one	me.
Return me not	y,
That I again	ay.

"The first bit has got to be 'Take me, Gemini,' " said Bottle. "And I suppose the last word might be 'day.' "

"That doesn't get us very far, does it?" I said. "There's a whole block in the middle that could say *anything*."

"You're right," said Bottle unhappily. "It's useless. What are we going to do now? You'll never get to your house without it."

"I'm going to use your telephone," I said. "And tell my mom everything. She'll know what to do for sure."

Bottle didn't argue this time. Down in the hall we dialed the number, and after a few rings my mom answered. Hearing her voice made me want to cry.

"555-5078."

"Mom. It's me."

"Hello?"

"Mom, it's me, Amy. I'm in a lot of trouble."

"Hello? 555-5078."

I turned to Bottle.

"She can't hear me," I said.

"Here, let me have a try," said Bottle, taking the receiver from me. I put my head up close so I could hear what was happening. "Hello. Is this Mrs. Settle?"

"Yes. Who is speaking please?"

"My name's Bottle. I'm Amy's friend. I . . ."

"I'll put her on. Amy . . . there's a friend of yours here. He says his name's Bottle . . . She's just coming . . . and *goodness* knows what she's done to her hair. . . . Here she is."

"Better still," said Bottle, covering the mouth-piece, "we can ask her for the spell. We'll have you home in no time."

"Hello, Castanetta," said Bottle. "It's me. Amy's mom obviously hasn't realized you're an imposter yet, luckily for you. I think you'd better tell me the spell, and we'll get you both back home at once."

Silence.

"Castanetta?"

"Castanetta, you'd better tell me, or I'll talk to Amy's mom and tell her to call the police."

Silence.

"Castanetta. Will you speak to me?"

It was when my mom came on the phone again that we began to realize what was happening.

"Hello," she said very loudly. "Can you hear me?"

"Yes," said Bottle. "I thought you were putting Amy on."

"I did," said Mom. "But she couldn't hear anything. I had the same problem when I first picked up the phone. There's obviously something wrong with it at the moment. Look, we're very busy here. Would you try again later please?"

The phone went dead.

"It's weird," said Bottle. "She can't hear you, and I can't hear Castanetta. . . . It's almost as if it's part of the spell. Even if your mom had let

me tell her what had happened to you, there would be no way of proving it."

"Perhaps Castanetta will tell my mom now that she knows you're on to her."

"Would she believe her?"

"No, I don't think she would. She's never even met a witch, and we certainly haven't got one in the family."

"So where does that leave you?"

"Trapped," I said. "Trapped in this house with a crazy witch."

Chapter Eleven

We turned to hear footsteps approaching the front of the house. A dark shape loomed behind the glass panes of the front door.

"Who is it?" I asked nervously.

Bottle shrugged.

"The mail carrier, I expect. We sometimes get a second delivery."

The doorbell rang.

"It must be a package," said Bottle. He pulled on the door handle, but as the witch had threatened, it was stuck fast. "Sorry," he called, hooking up the letter flap. "The door's stuck."

"Not to worry," said the mail carrier. "I think I can shove it through."

He forced a brown padded envelope into the slot, and Bottle tugged it through.

"There are a few bills, too," said the mail carrier, slipping them through after it.

"Please wait," I called, pushing Bottle out of the way and hooking the flap open again. "You've got to help me. I'm being kept here against my will by his grandma."

"Oh, dear me," laughed the mail carrier, posing in mock horror. "Is she a wicked witch?"

"Yes," I said urgently. "That's *exactly* what she is. Please, you've got to get help."

"Forget it, Amy," said Bottle. "It's no use."

The mail carrier bent down and pushed his face right up to the slot so that I could see the red veins in his eyes.

"If that's the case," he said, grinning, "I'd better call the police and the fire department, hadn't I? Do you think you'll need an ambulance, too?"

Bottle was right. It was no use. I watched the mail carrier walk off down the drive, shaking his head to himself and chuckling at his wonderful sense of humor.

"I could have told you not to bother with him," said Bottle.

"Because he's a grown-up?"

"No," said Bottle. "Because I'm beginning

to believe that the magic of the ring is so powerful that it will be impossible for you to get back in any way but the way that was intended."

"With the spell we don't have?"

"Yes. You tried to talk to your mother, but she didn't hear you. The mail carrier heard what you were saying, but he didn't understand. There's not much difference really, is there?"

He examined the padded envelope in his hand.

"It's for Castanetta and me," he said. "From Mom."

"Lucky you," I said. "I may never see *my* mom again."

"I'm sorry," he said. "You can read it with me if you like." And he smiled at me so nicely that I agreed.

We sat together on the bottom stair, and he eagerly tore the envelope open. There was a slim parcel inside addressed to Witch Ethel.

"That's odd," he said. "It had *our* names on the outside."

"There's a letter in there, too," I said. "Perhaps that will explain."

Dear Bottle and Castanetta,

I hope all is well with you and that you are remembering to feed yourselves properly. Life with Betishka is very hectic, as usual. She is just as kooky as ever, but she's really good company.

She insists on sending the enclosed computer disk for Grandma Ethel. I expect it gives details of healing remedies. I've tried to explain to her that Ethel is not the kind of witch she is, but, as ever, it is hard to get a word in edgewise. I wouldn't bother to

give the package to your grandma. It will only con-
fuse her. You might as well format the disk and use it
yourself.

Please water the plants, and don't forget to pay the
milkman. Take care of yourselves.

Much love,
Mom

P.S. I'm going shopping for presents for you today
while Betishka is with her patients.

"She sounds nice," I said. "Like my mom."

"She is," said Bottle. "But Aunt Betishka is
brilliant. This disk may be just the thing we
need."

"It may be what *you* need, but I'm certainly
not in the mood for playing with the computer."

"Who said anything about playing?" said
Bottle.

He opened the parcel and slid out a disk
labeled Betishka's Universal Spellmatic. With it
was a piece of yellow notepaper on which was
written:

Dear Witch Ethel,

Having heard about you from my sister Wendy, I thought the enclosed disk might interest you. Spellmatic covers numerous areas of witchcraft, including many of my own spells and remedies. I hope it will prove a useful aid to spreading good witch practices.

As yet unfinished is the Childsearch section of the program, designed to enable witches to help parents locate their lost children. Though I have made it possible to view the child on a monitor situated in the child's own home, I have yet to perfect a program that will run from any witch's study. Also, the program will be of little use unless an exact location of the child can be obtained.

I am working on this at present, and once it is finished, I hope the Spellmatic disk will be sold to registered witches worldwide. However, as a relative, you are very welcome to use this unfinished copy. Do let me know what you think.

Best wishes,
Betishka

"It's dynamite!" said Bottle, his eyes wide with excitement. "There's no way I'm going to format *this*."

"I think you should. Your mom trusts you."

"I'm not going to do anything bad with it. Don't you see? With Aunt Betishka's Child-search program we can see what Castanetta's up to. It might give us a clue how to get you back."

"But it's only meant for registered witches. It might be just as dangerous as your grandma's ring in the wrong hands."

"Do you want to go home or not?"

I nodded.

"Then it's a risk we'll have to take, isn't it?" asked Bottle.

We went up to his room. Bottle slid Betishka's disk into his disk drive and watched the screen closely as these words flashed up in huge red letters:

BETISHKA'S UNIVERSAL

SPELLMATIC

SPELLS AT YOUR

FINGERTIPS

The computer flickered and whirred a bit before producing this message:

ALL PROGRAMS AND

INFORMATION

RECORDED ON THIS DISK

ARE FOR THE USE OF

REGISTERED WITCHES

ONLY

Along the bottom of the screen was a set of possible commands. Bottle pressed Escape, Transfer, Load and got a message saying, Enter Filename or Press F1 to Select from List.

"It's not too late to format it," I said.

But Bottle had already pressed the key to reveal an alphabetical list. He scrolled down it past entries such as Anxiety, Aroma-Therapy,

Balm, Barley Water, and Chilblains until the cursor rested over Childsearch.

"Let's see what Castanetta's up to, shall we?" he said.

He pressed Enter to reveal the following instructions:

COMPLETE THE FOLLOWING:
surname of child
first name of child
child's date of birth
surname of father
first name of father
father's date of birth
surname of mother if different from above
first name of mother
mother's date of birth
address (including country)
check your answers, then press spacebar

Bottle completed the questions and pressed the spacebar.

"I don't believe a computer can find somebody with only that to go on," I said.

"You're right," said Bottle. "It says, 'Place a possession of the child's against screen for one minute. Items such as clothing or a favorite soft toy are particularly effective.' "

"This has got to be a joke," I said. "Computers don't work like that."

"No," said Bottle, "but *magic* does."

He fetched one of Castanetta's socks and pressed it against the screen.

"Time me, would you?" he said. "It has to be a full minute."

I was still protesting about how ridiculous the whole thing was when Castanetta's face appeared on the screen behind her sock, looking as clear as if she were on the other side of a pane of glass.

Chapter Twelve

*W*atching Castanetta was like watching a well-filmed program on a good color television. She was in *my* bedroom, lying on *my* bed, eating *my* apple, and reading *my* magazine.

"Look at her," I said angrily. "She's acting like she owns the place."

The picture moved around to show her from a different angle.

"And look at the state of my room! She's been snooping in all the drawers. My mom will have something to say when she sees that."

As if on cue, Mom came into the room, along with my brother, Toby.

"I want a word with you," she said to Castanetta.

"Want word," said Toby, rolling himself up in the end of my comforter.

Castanetta lowered her magazine.

"What about?" she said rudely, with her mouth full of apple.

"About you running up to your room while I was still talking to you," said Mom. "And about your hair. Whatever do you mean by messing about with it? You've straightened out all your lovely curls."

"Mess," said Toby from inside the comforter.

"And look at the state of your room," said Mom, running her hand through her hair. "This isn't at all like you, Amy. It looks as if a whirlwind has been through it."

"Whirlynd, whirlynd," said Toby. He untangled himself, jumped onto a pile of clothes, and threw a handful of socks into the air.

"I'll expect this to be cleaned before lunch," said Mom.

Castanetta said nothing.

"Do you hear me?" said Mom.

"As a matter of fact," said Castanetta, taking another bite of my apple, "I was just going out to play. And don't bother with lunch for me. I'm not hungry."

Mom stood openmouthed as Castanetta sauntered past her and out of the room.

"How *dare* she talk to my mom like that!" I said angrily. "Just wait until I see your precious Castanetta again. I'll have one or two things to say to her."

"Sorry," said Bottle. "I don't know what's the matter with her. She's always being nasty to *me*, but our mom would never let her behave like that."

"She probably thinks she can get away with it because it's someone else's mom," I said bitterly.

The Childsearch picture followed Castanetta out into the garden. She went over to my hiding place, where she sat with her back to the wall, pulling leaves off the laurel bush.

"Why did the ring have to bring me to *this* dump?" she said to herself. "It's nearly as bad as home. And I'm probably stuck here forever."

A head appeared above the wall behind her. It was James Bone.

"She better watch out," I said to Bottle. "That's James Bone. He's a menace."

"Hello, Amy Settle," said James, far too politely.

Castanetta didn't bother to look around.

"Bug off, whoever you are," she said.

"I told you I'd be back," said James. "And I've got something for you."

Castanetta looked mildly interested.

"What is it?" she said.

"A present, just for you."

"Hand it over then," said Castanetta, pulling a few more leaves off my laurel bush. "*Then* bug off."

James Bone looked disappointed.

"He won't like that," I said to Bottle. "He finds bullying much more fun if people put up a fight."

"OK," said James, shrugging. "You asked for it."

He pulled a loaded water pistol from each pocket, leaned over the wall above her, and squirted water all over her head and shoulders until both water pistols were empty.

Castanetta was speechless.

"That's just for starters," said James Bone. "I'll be back later."

And he sped off on his skateboard.

Chapter Thirteen

Suddenly we heard the witch's voice, calling from the landing.

"Bottle," she said, her voice strangely sweet. "Would you come here please?"

"Oh no," I said. "What does *she* want."

"She must have seen through our demon story," said Bottle. "And now she wants to get her own back."

I pressed the Escape key and the alphabetical list reappeared on the screen.

"Bottle!" called the witch.

"What did you do that for?" said Bottle.

"She might come and get you," I said. "And I don't think this is a good time for her to discover that I really *am* an intruder, do you?"

"You're right," said Bottle anxiously. "Things are bad enough without that."

He turned to the door.

We listened.

"Bottle," called the witch. "You'd better come at once, or there'll be trouble."

"Why do you think she's calling you and not me?" I said.

"She's up to something," said Bottle. "She wants to separate us."

"Or perhaps she *has* realized I'm an intruder."

"I'm coming to get you, Bottle," called the witch. "Now."

"Whatever it is," I said, "you'd better go."

"I suppose so," said Bottle. And, reluctantly, he left.

I sat, staring hopelessly at the computer screen, expecting at any moment to hear cries of anguish coming from the witch's room. I made my eyes focus on the list and began to read out the entries, Anxiety, Aroma-Therapy, Balm, Barley Water, Chilblains, Childsearch, Coughs, speaking very slowly and calmly to keep my mind off what the witch might be doing to Bottle.

When I had read all the entries on the screen, I pressed the Page Down key to reveal some more: Dandruff, Gout, Headaches, Indigestion. I moved down the list reading on and on until something unusual in the S section caught my attention. It said Spellpast. The Gemini ring used a spell from the past. Was there a chance of finding the words I needed to get home?

I put the cursor over Spellpast and pressed Enter, and the following warning appeared on the screen:

THESE SPELLS AND

CHANTS

ARE FOR THE HISTORICAL

REFERENCE OF

<u>REGISTERED WITCHES</u>

ONLY AND

<u>MUST NOT BE USED</u>

After some whirring noises, a list appeared with entries like these:

ANCIENT SPELLS AND

CHANTS

BROOMSTICK COMMANDS

CAULDRON CARE

LOTIONS

POTIONS

WITCH LORE

I put the cursor over Ancient Spells and Chants and pressed Enter to reveal a long list of spell names. I scrolled straight to G, but there was no mention of Gemini.

"Darn it," I said. "I'm going to be stuck here forever."

But my finger kept on scrolling, and there, under R, was the word Rings. I put the cursor over it and pressed Enter.

I found the Gemini rhyme easily. It was the third on the list. It read as follows:

Take me, Gemini, o'er land and sea,

To the one who most resembles me.

Return me not until the day,

That I again your name do say.

Underneath was this historical information:

As with many seemingly harmless
magic rings, the Gemini ring could
prove very dangerous. On the outward
journey it was extremely effective and
would speedily take the owner to a
look-alike. However, if during the visit
the look-alike innocently wore the
Gemini ring and read the inscription
aloud, she would be taken back to the
owner's home. Unless the look-alike
also had knowledge of the Gemini
rhyme both she and the owner could
be trapped in each other's lives forever.

The use of such rings was therefore
banned in Victorian times.

The Gemini ring was still on my finger. The rhyme was on the screen. I suppose I could have gone home immediately. It was very tempting. But Bottle had been kind to me. What if he was in danger? What if he needed me? He'd risked everything to help me get the Gemini ring. I couldn't just desert him. And even if he was all right, it would only be polite to wait and say good-bye to him.

I picked up a pen and copied the rhyme on a small piece of paper, which I put safely, with the Gemini ring, in my pocket. I decided to wait in Bottle's room for five more minutes, and if he hadn't returned by then I would go and investigate.

While I was waiting for him I had a look at a few more spells. I didn't think it would hurt. It wasn't as if I'd ever use them.

Chapter Fourteen

Five minutes later I met Bottle on the landing.

"I was just coming to get you," he said.

"Is everything all right? I was beginning to get worried."

"Everything's fine," he said. "I think."

"What do you mean?"

"I mean that Grandma's being nice."

"How odd."

"That's what I thought. She actually smiled at me. I went in there expecting to be turned into a boll weevil again and was smiled at. Can you imagine it? Her face was all rotten teeth and withered lips. It gave me the creeps."

"What did she actually want . . . the name of a good dentist?"

"She wanted to invite us in for a snack. She

said she had something to celebrate and would be honored if we would join her."

"Ugh! I bet it'll be bat's blood and centipede sandwiches."

"That's what I thought, but after I rearranged her room she sent me down to get something normal from the refrigerator. I hadn't realized how hungry I was until I looked in there. We've got ginger ale, bread, and lots of cheese."

"Do you think she's up to something?"

"I don't know, but I wouldn't like to risk turning down her invitation. She's weird when she's being nice, but it's better than when she's mad."

"I still don't like the sound of it," I said. "There's something I think you ought to do before we go in there. Come back to your room and I'll explain."

But it was too late. The witch's door opened and her wizened face peered round.

"Come in, dears," she said sweetly. "I'm ready for you now."

The witch ushered us in and shut the door. The room, lit by a single candle, was hot and close and still smelled dreadfully of smoke.

"Here we are," she said. "I got Bottle to clear my table and put it in the middle of the room so we can all sit around it. Doesn't it look nice?"

On the table was a plate of bread and cheese, a tub of margarine, a jar of pickles, a large bottle of ginger ale, three knives, and three glasses.

"Make yourselves comfy on the edge of my bed," said the witch. "And I'll sit over here."

We sat stiffly on her filthy bedspread. At the top of the bed, lying in a dip in the witch's greasy pillow, lay the cat, its yellow eyes half-open.

"Don't worry about him," said the witch. "He's useless."

She pulled her chair up to the opposite side of the table and sat.

"Isn't this nice?" said the witch. Her mouth was smiling all right, but her eyes were as mean and hard as ever. "I expect you're wondering what we are about to celebrate."

We said nothing. She was going to tell us anyway.

"The visit of the demons, which could easily have been a disaster for me, has led me to a *very* exciting discovery. As you know, I have been working for years on a special recipe. When it is ready it will be superior to any potion ever invented. And it will prove that I . . . ," here she stood, " . . . am a Princess of Power, an Empress of Evil. . . . " She raised her arms into the air. "The Witch of All Witches."

"It must be quite a potion," said Bottle.

"It is," said the witch, sitting again. "It was some weeks ago, after years of research and experiment, that I realized I was getting close. I began to write details of the ingredients in my best recipe book and started to collect them together, always choosing those of the best possible quality. Since then I have mixed tiny amounts in here."

She bent under the table and produced her carved wooden bowl.

"By measuring and sifting, blending and smoothing, I have worked toward the perfect potion. I finished writing it this morning, but I still had a few ingredients to collect. When the last page of my recipe was burned I was horrified. I wasn't sure I could remember those last few items . . . and if I couldn't, the whole recipe would be ruined."

"Poor you," said Bottle, trying to hide his relief.

"That's what I thought," said the witch. "But how wrong I was. If it hadn't been for that beetle, I'd never have known."

She threw back her head and cackled.

"What beetle?" I said.

"A nice fat one I'd been saving for a snack," she said. "It must have escaped when the demons came. I found it scuttling around my table, but before I had time to catch it, it fell off into this bowl. I don't know why the lid was off. I always keep it on to prevent the cat from getting at it. The beetle struggled about in here for a bit, then, realizing that it had landed in something rather special, it began to eat. And that was when it happened."

"What happened?" said Bottle.

"It disappeared. Vanished. My recipe was ready, and I didn't need the missing page at all. I should have realized I'd got there yesterday when the mixture went transparent. What a silly witch I've been."

"So it's a potion to make people disappear?" said Bottle.

The witch nodded proudly.

"But surely witches have always been able to make people disappear," I said, trying not to sound rude.

"Yes, yes," said the witch impatiently. "But do you know that every one of those spells and potions they use is reversible? Imagine that. A witch thinks she's got rid of someone for good, obliterated them forever, and some nasty sneak of a goody-goody comes along and undoes the spell. It's all very unsatisfactory."

"So your mixture got rid of the beetle for good?" said Bottle.

"It did," said the witch excitedly. "I've tried

every reversal spell I know. But it's gone all right. It's as if it never existed in the first place."

"But why make such a potion?" said Bottle. "You won't be able to use it, will you? Dangerous potions like that were banned years ago."

"Banned?" said the witch. "What nonsense. Wherever did you get an idea like that? Why, when I was a girl—"

"But things have changed a lot since then," said Bottle. "My aunt Betishka's a witch, and she says—"

"And has your aunt Betishka heard of my new potion?" asked the witch.

"No."

"Has anybody heard of it, apart from the three of us?"

"No."

"Then it can't have been banned, can it?" said the witch, her eyes gleaming triumphantly.

"I suppose not," said Bottle unhappily.

"Good," said the witch. "Now let's celebrate. I'll pour the drinks while you help yourselves to food. Don't wait for me."

Although we hadn't eaten since breakfast, neither of us felt hungry anymore. The witch didn't seem to notice. She picked up the bottle of ginger ale and peered at the label.

"Ginger ale?" she said. "Never heard of it. It looks like cold tea to me. Couldn't you have found something more festive, Bottle? Perhaps I'll have some of my nettle wine instead."

She turned the cap on the bottle and jumped back, startled, when it fizzed in her face. She took a cautious sip from the bottle, then swigged some more.

"Not bad," she said. "It bubbles like a witch's brew. I think I'll have some after all."

She wiped the rim on her dirty cuff and poured ginger ale into each of the three glasses.

"Good. The drinks are ready," she said, allowing a sly expression to creep onto her face. "And now perhaps I'd better tell you why you're *really* here."

Chapter Fifteen

"I've just remembered something really important I've got to do," said Bottle, standing.

"And I've got to help him," I said, preparing to follow. "Perhaps you could tell us some other time."

"Not so fast," said the witch.

She rose from her chair and stood with her arms pointing toward us. Her gnarled fingers stuck out like withered tree roots and her eyes gleamed wickedly.

Her thin lips began to move, silently but rapidly, as she breathed evil words in our direction.

"My legs!" said Bottle. "They won't work. They've gone numb." He punched them with his fist to try to get the feeling back. "Let us out of here, you hag."

The witch's lips were still now, and Bottle slumped helplessly down on the bed beside me. I was relieved to find that *my* legs were not affected but decided this was not the time to let on to Bottle and the witch.

"Good," said the witch. "That should help you concentrate on what I've got to say. It only lasts for fifteen minutes, but that should give us plenty of time. It doesn't do to waste your energy on long spells at my age."

"You want to try your potion on us, don't you?" said Bottle, his voice taut with fear. "You want to see if it works on people as well as beetles."

"Very good," said the witch. "You're not as stupid as you look. What a pity I can't keep you. I suppose I could just give it to Castanetta, but then I'd always have the worry that you might tell someone my little secret. And that would never do, would it?"

"We're not trying it," I said. "You can't make us."

"Don't worry," said the witch. "You'll hardly notice it. If my work has been successful the mixture should be completely tasteless. And to help it down, I thought we'd mix it in a nice drink for you."

She took two of the glasses of ginger ale and, with a battered tablespoon, scooped a dollop of the mixture from her wooden bowl into each of them. The ginger ale fizzed up a bit, but once it settled down the three glasses looked identical.

"Here are your drinks," said the witch, placing one of the contaminated glasses in front of each of us.

And that was when I knew I had to do something. I felt in my pocket for the Gemini ring, slipped it on my finger, and stood dramatically. I pointed my arms at the startled witch, closed my eyes, and chanted the following spell:

Callera, mallera, dallera, dice,
Freeze, body, as stiff as ice.
See not, hear not, feel not, fear not,
Callera, mallera, dallera, dice.

When I opened my eyes I could see the witch leaning toward me across the table. Her face was drawn into a grotesque look of horror, and her arms reached out as if she would take me by the throat. I stepped back, terrified.

"It's all right, Amy," said Bottle. "You've frozen her. However did you manage that?"

"It was on your aunt Betishka's disk," I said, breathing again. "I had a look at one or two spells after she called you. Somehow that one stayed in my head. Your aunt Betishka's notes said it would work for anybody in possession of a magical trinket, whether they were a witch or not. She said it was important that the information should not get into the hands of ordinary members of the public. I know I shouldn't have looked at it, and I certainly didn't mean to use it. But it *was* an emergency, wasn't it?"

"Absolutely," said Bottle. "But that doesn't explain why Grandma's spell didn't work on your legs just now."

"There was something else," I said. "A special chant to protect me against evil spells for one full hour. I said it before I came to find you, just in case the witch was up to no good. That's what I was trying to tell you in the corridor. I thought you ought to say it, too."

"I wish I had," said Bottle. "My legs are useless. You'll have to help me get out of here."

"Of course, but we're not going until we've dealt with your grandma," I said. "Watch this."

I swapped Bottle's ginger ale glass with the witch's and tipped the contents of *my* glass into one of her police helmets. I then wiped the glass carefully with a tissue and refilled it with ordinary ginger ale.

"I think it's time we all drank a toast to your grandma's success," I said. "Don't you?"

"You're not going to bring her round, are you?" said Bottle. "What if she's been watching us? She'll be livid."

"If your aunt Betishka's notes are right, she won't remember a thing."

"And what if they're not right?" said Bottle.

Chapter Sixteen

I touched the witch's frozen fingertips and repeated the first line of the spell:

Callera, mallera, dallera, dice.

The witch returned to normal immediately and carried on talking as if nothing had happened.

"They thought I was no good when I was a young witch, you know," she said. "Just because I was slower than the others to learn my spells. And when I grew up they still laughed at me. But I've outlived the lot of them, and now my name will go down in history as the greatest witch of all time. Let's raise our glasses and drink a toast."

She picked up her glass, the glass that contained her own potion.

"Come along," she said. "You know you can't escape, so you may as well do as you're told."

"Won't you change your mind?" I said. "It's really very cruel to make us disappear when we've lived so little of our lives."

"Certainly not," she said. "Nobody cared about me when *I* was your age. Why should I care about you?"

"Please," said Bottle. "You might regret this toast."

"My mind is made up," said the witch. "And don't worry, I'll have used this on plenty of other people before my life's out. There's that man who had the audacity to come and build a house near my hovel for a start. I expect he thought I'd forget. But Witch Ethel never forgets. And then there is your precious mother. She had no right to bring me here. I'll deal with her all right."

"So we have no choice?" I said.

"No choice," said Bottle.

We picked up our glasses. The witch laughed triumphantly. Insanely.

"A toast," she said. "To *me*, the Witch of All Witches."

She raised her glass to her lips.

"Let's drink!"

We all drank. The witch, whose nastiness had obviously made her quite thirsty, drained her glass in three seconds flat. And then, still smiling, she disappeared.

"It's worked," said Bottle, amazed.

"What *have* we done?" I said, suddenly feeling guilty.

"We've done what she was going to do to us," said Bottle grimly.

"I can't help feeling bad, though."

"I'm afraid it was the only way to stop her," said Bottle. "And she definitely had to be stopped."

"Thank goodness I've got the Gemini ring," I said. "Imagine if she'd taken it with her."

Bottle's face clouded.

"But what if you can't complete the rhyme?" he said. "We should have forced her to tell us before she went."

"Don't worry," I said. "I've got it. I found it on your aunt Betishka's disk."

"Excellent," said Bottle. But then his expression turned to one of puzzlement. "But if you know the rhyme, why are you still here? I thought you couldn't wait to get back to your mom."

"I can't," I said. "And I'm really mad about what Castanetta has been saying to her and afraid of what she might have done to Toby. But I didn't want to go without saying goodbye . . . and anyway, I was a bit worried about what your grandma might be doing to you. I thought you might need help."

Bottle went a bit pink.

"Well," he said. "That's about the nicest thing anybody's ever done for me. . . . I don't think I know what to say."

He stood and walked as far as the door before he realized he had got the feeling back in his legs.

"Oh, wow!" he said, flinging the door open. "Let's get out of here forever."

It was tempting. Bright shafts of sunshine beamed enticingly into the room, their insides swirling with clouds of ancient dust.

"Not until we decide how to get rid of this," I said, pointing at the wooden bowl.

"Yes," said Bottle, "and this." He picked up the recipe book. "In fact, let's get rid of as much as we can. It's all dangerous. I think it's time to light the barbecue at the bottom of the garden.

We can leave anything that won't fit in there in her room, and Mom can deal with it when she gets back."

"Are you allowed to use the barbecue?"

"No," he admitted. "Mom always makes me keep away from it when it's burning."

"What we need is a spell that will light a fire from a distance and put it out in a second," I said.

"Don't tell me," he laughed. "You just happened to see one on Aunt Betishka's disk."

I nodded. "But I think it should be the last one we use," I said.

Something moved at the head of the bed. It was the thin black cat. It stood, stretched stiffly, and stared at us with knowing yellow eyes.

"You don't think *he* has powers, do you?" said Bottle nervously.

"I hope not," I said.

The cat padded down the filthy bed toward me. He stepped onto my lap, pressed his thin body against me, and looked up sadly into my face.

"It's all right," I said, stroking his bony head. "He's just a pussycat that needs cuddling."

"He looks as if he could do with a meal, too,"

said Bottle. "He's probably been living on cock-roaches for years."

Later, we stood in the back garden. Down by the far wall the barbecue burned steadily, sending into the air foul black smoke that would infuriate the neighbors. And under a laurel bush the thin black cat, who had just enjoyed a meal of cold sausage and fresh milk from the refrigerator, played with a long grass stem.

The Gemini ring was still on my finger. I took the piece of paper from my pocket and prepared to read the spell.

"Bye," said Bottle, shuffling from one foot to another. "And thanks."

"Bye."

"Don't forget to send Castanetta back, will you?"

"Of course not . . . and you know what to do the minute you see her?"

"Throw this in the barbecue," said Bottle, holding up Aunt Betishka's Universal Spellmatic disk.

"What will you tell your mom?" I said. "About where your grandma's gone."

"The truth, I think," said Bottle. "She always finds out in the end."

"You've got my address," I said. "You could write."

"Yes," said Bottle.

But we both knew that he wouldn't.

"Bye."

"Bye."

I read the spell:

> Take me, Gemini, o'er land and sea,
> To the one who most resembles me.
> Return me not until the day,
> That I again your name do say.

And once more I felt the strange tingling sensation that spread from my toes to my head. Bottle began to fade from view, growing smaller and dimmer as I moved away. It was slow at first, then faster and faster, as I whizzed away from Adderwort at great speed. Colors, noises, and blurred shapes flashed past me, but there was nothing I could make out until, a few minutes later, I flopped down onto hard mud between the laurel bush and the wall in our front garden.

Chapter Seventeen

Sitting next to me was Castanetta. And beside her were the two Squeaky Clean bottles and a big plastic shopping bag.

"How did *you* get back?" she said rudely.

"With the ring, of course," I said. "But I'd never have managed it if Bottle hadn't helped me. Your grandma magicked it off my finger as soon as I got there."

"That's what I was worried about," said Castanetta, pulling more leaves off the laurel bush.

Looking more closely, I could see grimy streaks on her face, as if she had been crying.

"I thought you *wanted* to swap places," I said.

"I did," said Castanetta. "But that was before your mom started nagging me. She wouldn't let me have lunch, you know. She's cruel."

"Perhaps she wanted you to tidy up the mess you'd made," I said.

Castanetta gave me a sharp look.

"I've cleaned it now," she said. "And I've apologized. But she says I've got to wait until dinner."

"Well, if it's any comfort to you," I said, "*I* haven't eaten, either."

I took off the Gemini ring and held it out to her.

"I think you'll be needing this," I said.

Castanetta hesitated.

"But what will Grandma do to me? I didn't collect the things she wanted."

The fear on her face almost made her look human.

"I wouldn't worry about *her*," I said. "That's all been dealt with. But I think you owe Bottle an apology. It sounds as if he's been covering for you for ages."

"Do you think he'll be angry with me?"

"Probably," I said. "But not for long. I would think he's a pretty good brother to have, isn't he?"

Castanetta nodded.

She put on the Gemini ring and we quickly

changed clothes, hoping that nobody would look over the wall and see us.

"You're going to be in trouble with your mom," she said awkwardly. "And I think I may have put some things away in the wrong places in your room. . . . And I just wanted to say—"

"I know," I said grimly. "You're sorry."

"But at least you'll be ready for James Bone," she said, grinning suddenly. "The bottles are full of very cold water, and I've put some special back-up ammunition in the bag."

I peered into the bag to see six balloons, each full of water.

"Water balloons," she said. "Make them burst on the pavement at his feet. That'll get him danc-ing."

"When's he due?" I said.

"Any minute now."

I crouched against the wall and slowly slid upward to peep over it. Gliding toward us on his skateboard came James Bone, balancing a large red bucket precariously in his hands.

"He's coming," I said. "You take the balloons, and I'll handle the bottles."

Castanetta was a great shot. The first balloon burst right in front of James's skateboard. He lost his balance, stepped awkwardly off his skate-board, and spilled the water from the red bucket all over his feet. The second balloon landed behind him, and the others rained all around him, two bursting and two rolling down to the gutter along with his bucket.

"Thanks for the ammunition," said James, swiftly retrieving the undamaged balloons.

He lobbed them back, but they still wouldn't burst.

"Quick, Castanetta," I said. "Chuck them back again."

"Don't try that old trick of pretending there's more than one of you," said James, laughing. "Nobody but you would be fool enough to take *me* on."

"Show him, Castanetta," I cried, holding the Squeaky Clean bottles at the ready.

But there was no answer. Castanetta had gone.

I gulped.

"There *was* someone else," I said feebly, noticing a loaded water pistol sticking out of each of James's trouser pockets. "But she's gone home."

James took out his water pistols.

I held my Squeaky Clean bottles.

We stood facing each other, like cowboys in a Western. Waiting.

"So it's just you and me," said James, sneering.

"It looks like it," I said. "But there's something I'd like to say first."

"Yeah? What?"

"It's great to see you again."